CUENTO
DE LUZ

FSC
www.fsc.org
MIX
Paper from
responsible sources
FSC® C007923

Little Chick and Mommy Cat

Text © 2012 Marta Zafrilla
Illustrations © 2012 Nora Hilb
This edition © 2012 Cuento de Luz SL
Calle Claveles 10 | Urb Monteclaro | Pozuelo de Alarcón | 28223 Madrid | Spain | www.cuentodeluz.com
Original title in Spanish: Hijito Pollito
English translation by Jon Brokenbrow
2nd printing
ISBN: 978-84-15241-96-6

Printed by Shanghai Chenxi Printing Co., Ltd., in PRC, November 2012, print number 1323

Little Chick and Mommy Cat

Marta Zafrilla
Nora Hilb

My school friends haven't got a clue.
My mommy is a cat, and I'm a chick.
So what's the big deal? She can't have
kittens, and a hen who couldn't feed all
of her chicks asked her if she wanted
me. And she said yes! I was only an egg,
but she looked after me as if I were
her own.

At first, I thought I was a cat, too,
because my Mommy's a beautiful cat
and all of my neighbors are cats.
I wanted to meow, run around,
lick my paws, and flick my ears
with my tail, but I couldn't!

One day, Mommy told me that I would never be like other cats because my birth mother was a hen. I would never have four paws, but one day, I'd be able to fly with my little wings.

Mommy promised to teach me everything she knew so I could grow up like a cat, and to tell you the truth, I was soon happy to be the only half-cat, half-chick in the city.

Mommy and I live in an attic in Meowburg. There are a lot of cats around Mommy, but she says that for the time being there's only one flying cat in her life. She always tells me to be careful, because despite being accepted as one of the guys, I'm still a tasty morsel for all of the cats on our street.

The fact is, when we go out for a stroll, we feel like people are looking at us. At first it bugged me and I'd say, "Mommy, why are they looking at us like that?"

"Because we're different, honey," she'd say.

"And is it bad to be different?" I'd ask.

"No, not at all; it's bad if you want to be like everyone else!" she'd explain.

"That's so boring!" I'd say. "I want to be original!"

And since then, I don't care if people point at us.

In the park, all of the kittens are happy to play with me. Because they're so small and still a little clumsy, though, I've come home a few times with less feathers than I'd like!

Mommy's always watching out in case I end up in the mouth of some greedy cat, but I'm getting stronger and I've learned to defend myself.

Especially since I learned how to fly!

It's not always easy being a chick.

My neighbor Catty is madly in love with me, precisely, she says, because I'm not a cat. Girls are crazy! I like Catty a lot, but sometimes she gets so carried away that I have to run away and hide from her!

Mommy decided that although I was growing up with cats, I should be educated as a chick. My school is a long way from home—a long, long way away.

It's a big effort for her, but every day Mommy carries me on her back to the Bird School on Wingburg Street. There I learn everything I need to know about being a chicken. (Let's be honest, Mommy can't help me much with that, because she's a cat!)

Mommy soon realized that I'd never learn to meow or jump, no matter how hard I tried at the Cat School.

And I tried ever so hard, but I just couldn't do it. With a beak and two dinky feet like mine, I'll never be a real cat.

But it doesn't bother me.

Really, I'm happy to be a chick.

At school, people still look at me,
even though we're all chicks.

When we leave school and all the moms
are there with our snacks in their beaks,
Chicky always asks me, "Is that really
your mom? She hasn't got a beak!"
And I say to him, "No, she hasn't, and
she doesn't know how to cluck, either.
But she's got a mouth to meow me
beautiful lullabies."

Lily, who's the smallest one in my class, always says to me in flying lessons: "Is it true your mommy can't fly?"

"No," I say, "she can't fly, she walks. And you know something else? She hasn't got feathers, but instead she's got soft, glossy fur that I cuddle into when I'm cold."

And Chucky, the most talkative of my friends, said to me the other day in corn counting class: "Did you say your Mom has got a long, long tail?" And I said, "Yes, it's great! It flicks away all of the flies in summer!"

One day, my best friend Checky came back to my house and said, "Is that your real Mom? She's got four legs, and you've only got two!"
And I said to him, "Of course, four are better than two! My Mommy can run really fast, especially when I fall down and she comes over to pick me up."
Checky wanted to see for himself, and after dinner we had a great time when Mommy took him home, riding on her back.

Not only the kids are surprised that I'm a chick and Mommy is a cat. Even my teacher, Mrs. Wattles, asked me in class one day, "Is that your mother? Why, she's got whiskers!" And I said to her, "Mrs. Wattles, I love my Mommy's whiskers! She uses them to tickle me!"

So you see, I don't mind when people ask me funny questions, but I don't understand why they're so surprised.

I know that most chicks have moms who are hens, that puppies have dads who are dogs, elephants have families who are all elephants, and ants have baby ants, but then there are families that are different.

Mine might be a bit strange, but I think it's the best family in the world!

I'm a chick, and my Mommy is a cat. And I love her!